The Night of the Ooley Bugs

For
Robert E. Mitchell,
my colleague

The Night of the Ooley Bugs

A Story by Noodles

with Goblins by James Endicott

HOLT, RINEHART AND WINSTON, PUBLISHERS
New York, Toronto, London, Sydney

Hissssssst!
Hissssssst!
Don't make a sound!

The ooley bugs are out of the ground...

One night a year –
tonight's the night! –

they frolic in the full-moon light...

They turn themselves inside out

and let a gang of goblins out...

Behind that tree!

See there!
See there!

That shadow moved!

Beware! Beware!

Down! Quick!
Into the grass

and let the wild oolies pass!

They're on the hunt...
They're prowling now...

Hear them grunt...
They're scowling now...

They have sharp teeth...

Their eyes are keen...

Their tempers are short...

Their claws are mean...

Stay hidden!
Stay hidden!
Don't be seen...

This is the night of in-between...

It's the ooley bugs'